Reading
BOROUGH COUNCIL

Reading Borough Libraries

Email: info@readinglibraries.org.uk
Website: www.readinglibraries.org.uk

Reading 0118 9015950
Battle 0118 9015100
Caversham 0118 9015103
Palmer Park 0118 9015106
Southcote 0118 9015109
Tilehurst 0118 9015112
Whitley 0118 9015115

SYMES, Ruth
Cornflake The Dragon

PET

To avoid overdue charges please return this book to a
Reading library on or before the last date stamped above.
If not required by another reader, it may be renewed by
personal visit, telephone, post, email, or via our website.

RUTH SYMES would like to have a small dragon
for a pet (or even a well-behaved big one). She
lives in Bedfordshire and when she isn't writing
she can be found by the river walking her dogs,
Traffy and Bella (who are often in the river).

Find out more at:

www.ruthsymes.com

Also by Ruth Symes

The **Bella Donna** series

Coven Road
Too Many Spells
Witchling
Cat Magic
Witch Camp
Bella Bewitched

The **Secret Animal Society** series

Cornflake the Dragon
Spike the Sea Serpent (March 2015)
. . . and even more exciting adventures
coming soon

The Secret Animal Society

CORNFLAKE
The Dragon

by Ruth Symes

Illustrated by Tina Macnaughton

Piccadilly

First published in Great Britain in 2014 by Piccadilly Press
Northburgh House, 10 Northburgh Street, London EC1V 0AT

Text copyright © Ruth Symes 2014
Illustrations copyright © Tina Macnaughton 2014

A CIP catalogue record for this book is available from the British Library.

ISBN: 978-1-84812-418-9

1 3 5 7 9 10 8 6 4 2

Printed and bound by Clays Ltd, St Ives Plc

www.piccadillypress.co.uk

Piccadilly Press is part of the Bonnier Publishing Group
www.bonnierpublishing.com

For Shania, Elizabeth, Isabel, Jessica, Sophia and Leyvi,
and for Thomas, who loves dragons xx

With thanks to Ruth Williams,
editor of the Bella Donna series, and Cornflake's first
fan xx

A letter from the author . . .

Dear Reader,

Thank you so much for looking inside this book. I loved writing it and hope you enjoy reading it. ☺

Did you know that there are hundreds and hundreds of dragon myths and legends? I like the ones about dragons' breath making clouds in the sky and dragons granting wishes best.

Plus, did you know that real-life Komodo dragons use their tongues to smell and tiny sea-dragon dads carry the baby eggs on their tails? Dragons truly are amazing.

Better go now as it's time for our breakfast. My dogs are having dog food and my husband's having toast but can you guess what my favourite breakfast is . . . it's cornflakes! ☺

Ruth.

www.secretanimalsociety.com

CHAPTER 1

When Miss Harper announced that the children in her class had been chosen to take care of the school pets for the summer holidays, everyone wanted to take one home.

'Me, Miss! Can I take the mice? *Pleeeease.*'

'How many carrots a day can the rabbit eat?'

'Oh, stick insects! Perfect . . .'

'Do hamsters like watching TV?'

Twins Izzie and Eddie were desperate to look after a pet, too – any of the animals would do.

'Looking after a school pet for the summer holidays is a very important job,' Miss Harper said. 'Can anyone look after the grass snake?'

Eddie's and Izzie's hands shot up like lightning.

'Kevin,' Miss Harper said, picking a boy in the back row. 'You can look after the grass snake. I'll give you a permission slip for your parents to sign.'

'Yes!' said Kevin. He punched his fist in the air as Eddie and Izzie sighed and put their hands slowly back down.

Eddie and Izzie weren't the only children not to be chosen to take any of the school pets home, but they *were* the most disappointed.

'Those of you who are taking care of school pets, make sure you bring them back on the first day of term,' Miss Harper told the class as the bell rang on the last day of term.

Most of the children stampeded straight

out of the classroom ready for the summer holidays. Eddie and Izzie were the last to leave.

'Who's taking the library lizard home?' the caretaker asked as he walked into the classroom, carrying a plastic tank and a packet of lizard pellets.

Miss Harper gulped. 'Oh dear, I forgot all about him!'

Eddie and Izzie were almost at the classroom door but now they stopped.

The library lizard lived on the windowsill at the back of the library. Usually it was hard to see him because the windowsill was piled high with books. The librarian had told Eddie and Izzie that he was a very grumpy lizard and he didn't like children –

or anyone else for that matter. But Eddie
and Izzie didn't mind.

'We'll look after him, Miss,' said Eddie.

'We're very good at looking after animals,'
said Izzie.

Miss Harper bit her bottom lip. Although

she liked Eddie and Izzie very much and was sure they were good, kind, pet-loving children, she hadn't got their parents' permission to send an animal home with them.

But if Eddie and Izzie didn't take the library lizard home with them, then she would have to, and she really didn't want to.

'Promise you'll take very good care of him?' she asked. 'If there's a problem ask your parents to call and I'll come to collect him.'

'We will,' Izzie promised.

Eddie peered into the tank. It had pebbles along the bottom and some plants around the edges. All he could see was a slime-green-

coloured tail sticking out of the ornamental cave in the centre of the tank.

'How old is he?' Eddie asked.

Miss Harper looked at the caretaker and the caretaker scratched his head.

'Old,' he said.

'Yes,' Miss Harper agreed. 'He was already here when I came to work at the school and that was five years ago.'

'Very old for a pet lizard,' the caretaker added. 'Might not . . .' He looked at Miss Harper.

She nodded. 'He's a very old lizard, so don't worry if he doesn't wake up one day,' she told the children.

Eddie caught a glimpse of the creature as it poked its head out of the cave and then quickly pulled it back again.

'I bet it's sad,' Eddie said.

'Oh, I don't think so,' said Miss Harper. 'He's just a lizard, after all. He doesn't have feelings. He sleeps a lot and doesn't move around much.'

But Eddie didn't agree with her. He thought he'd probably end up sleeping from boredom too if he were stuck in a prison for five whole years. A lifetime for a lizard.

'Did you know lobsters can live for hundreds of years?' he asked Miss Harper.

'No,' Miss Harper said. 'Are you sure?' It didn't sound likely but she wasn't really listening and she didn't see Eddie nod. She was checking she had her car keys in her bag. It was time to go.

'What's his name, Miss?' Izzie asked her.

But Miss Harper didn't know that either and nor did the caretaker. 'I don't think he has one. Tell you what, see if you can think of one for him over the summer holidays?'

'We will,' said Izzie. Her mind was already busy with possibilities: Logan, Loxy, Lively. Although the lizard didn't seem very lively.

Eddie picked up the tank.

'Have a good summer,' Miss Harper called after them, as she watched them go.

CHAPTER 2

Izzie and Eddie took it in turns to carry the lizard's tank. The further they went, the heavier the tank seemed to get.

'My arms are just about falling off,' Izzie groaned.

'Mine too,' said Eddie, as they turned the corner for Willow View flats.

'Oh, at last!' Izzie said when she saw the

grubby grey concrete tower block looming in front of them. 'Almost home.'

She looked into the tank just as the lizard came out of the ornamental cave and glared at her through the plastic.

'Oh my!' said Izzie.

'What is it?' Eddie asked her.

'His eyes are golden, like flames.'

Eddie looked into the tank too. 'He doesn't look very happy.'

'You wouldn't be happy if you were being bounced around in a plastic tank,' Izzie said. She put the tank on the ground. 'I'm getting him out.'

'What if he bites you?' Eddie said.

'Then I'll get bitten,' Izzie told him. She felt angry on the lizard's behalf. 'What harm can he do? He can only have tiny teeth – if he's got any teeth at all!'

Eddie didn't think the school would have poisonous pets or ones that could hurt children, so he reckoned they were probably safe enough. He watched as Izzie reached in. The lizard was about the length of her hand.

'Careful.'

Izzie carefully took hold of the lizard and cradled him against her spotty lilac T-shirt. 'Keep still now. We don't want you falling and hurting yourself,' she told him.

Eddie pushed the lift button on the ground floor of the block of flats and picked up the tank. The lift creaked and squeaked its way down to them.

'Thank goodness it's working again,' Eddie said.

That morning it had been broken and they'd had to walk down twenty flights of

stairs. He hadn't fancied walking back up them, and especially not while carrying the lizard's tank.

They were just about to get in the lift when their neighbour, Mrs Winters, came hurrying into the block, carrying three overflowing bags of groceries.

'Wait for me!' she called out. 'Don't you dare go until I'm there.'

Mrs Winters was always banging on their wall saying the TV was too loud or that they were being too noisy. She even complained when they played outside in the corridor between the two flats.

'Children should be seen and not heard,' she often said. Mrs Winters loved complaining.

Eddie waited until she'd got in too, and

then he pressed the button for the top floor. He had to be careful he didn't drop the tank as he did so.

'What's that?' Mrs Winters asked, staring at the tank. 'Not much room in here with it taking up so much space. It looks like a vivarium.'

The lizard's tank was taking up much less space than all of Mrs Winters' bags but Eddie didn't say so.

'What's a viv– vivarium?' he asked.

'A tank for keeping reptiles and amphibians in. Have you got something in it? You know you're not allowed to keep pets at Willow View flats. I'll have to report you if you do. It's my duty as a concerned citizen.'

Eddie was glad the creature wasn't still in the tank. 'It's empty,' he said truthfully. 'Look!'

He didn't dare glance over at Izzie in case Mrs Winters saw her holding the lizard. Izzie stared down at the ground and Mrs Winters' fuchsia pink shoes.

'Willow View has never allowed pets,' Mrs Winters continued. 'There used to be a sign up. One man had a canary and, well . . . he got evicted.'

Eddie and Izzie looked at each other in horror. They'd never seen any signs and they hadn't known about the No Pets rule.

Izzie looked down at the lizard cradled to her T-shirt and her mouth fell open in surprise. The lizard wasn't slime-green-coloured like he had been in his tank any more. Now he was exactly the same lilac colour and spotty pattern as her T-shirt. No wonder Mrs Winters hadn't noticed him – he was very hard to see.

The lift groaned and shuddered and made a pinging sound. They'd reached the top floor.

Mrs Winters bustled out first with her shopping and Eddie and Izzie followed after her.

'Lucky she didn't see him,' Eddie said.

'It wasn't luck,' Izzie told him. 'Look!'

Eddie looked at the lilac lizard and grinned. 'He's camouflaged himself,' he told Izzie as he rang their doorbell. 'You know, disguised himself so he blends in with the background. Like a chameleon – but he's definitely not a chameleon.'

'Do you think he disguised himself on purpose?' Lizzie said.

Eddie shook his head. 'He couldn't be that clever could he?'

'I'm just very glad he did,' Izzie said.

CHAPTER 3

'Warra-you-gor?' asked Eddie and Izzie's almost-three-year-old brother, Toby, when he opened the front door. As always, he had a partly chewed strawberry jam sandwich in his hand. He looked at the plastic tank Eddie was holding and the spotty lilac lump Izzie was cradling.

'Hello, you two, did you have a good day?'

Mum said, coming out of the tiny kitchen and down the passage to greet them.

'Warr-is-it?' Toby said and he poked a jammy finger at the lump.

'No!' Izzie squeaked as she spun away from him.

'Izzie?' Mum said.

The lizard jumped out of Izzie's arms and raced along the passage.

'A rat!' Mum screamed.

'It's not a rat!' Izzie shouted back as she and Eddie ran after the lizard. He was very fast but fortunately he hadn't had time to change colour and was still lilac, so they could easily see him on the worn green carpet.

'Not a rat?' Mum said, as she picked up Toby and his sandwich and followed them.

'It's as fast as a rat. What's going on, you two?'

The lizard ran along the skirting board. Izzie and Eddie ran down the passage to the kitchen, with Toby and Mum following them.

'Where can he have gone?' said Izzie.

'I can't see him anywhere,' said Eddie.

'But *what* was it?' Mum said.

'The library lizard,' Eddie said, looking under the cooker. 'We said we'd look after him for the holidays.'

'But I thought you two weren't chosen to look after any of the school pets,' Mum said.

'We weren't – but they forgot about the library lizard,' Eddie told her.

'We promised we'd take care of him and now we've lost him already!' Izzie said as she checked under the fridge.

'We'll find him,' Eddie told her, looking in the bin. 'He has to be in the flat somewhere.'

'But what if he gets hurt? What if he escapes?' Izzie said, and Mum heard the panic in her voice.

'We won't let that happen,' she told her firmly. 'Although I wish you'd been asked to look after something that moved slower – like a guinea pig.'

'Like Twinky?' Eddie said. Mum often told them about the guinea pig she'd had as a girl.

'Yes,' Mum said, smiling, but then she thought of something else. 'We'd better check high up on the walls and ceiling too. Lizards can climb!'

The flat only had one bedroom where Izzie and Eddie and Toby slept. Mum and Dad slept on a sofa bed in the lounge. Toby trundled off to the children's bedroom and Eddie went to check the bathroom as Izzie looked in the lounge.

Toby sat down on the floor next to his bed and had a bite of his sandwich. Then he looked into the darkness under his bed.

Under the bed was usually the home of forgotten socks, bits of sandwich and toys, but now it was also the hiding place of a golden-eyed lizard that blinked at him.

'Here, want san'wick?' Toby said.

The lizard scuttled further under the bed.

When Eddie and Izzie came into the room, Toby pointed to where the lizard was hiding and then put his finger to his mouth.

The twins crouched down and looked. They could see the lizard's fiery eyes staring back at them but they couldn't reach him.

'We'll have to move the bed,' Eddie said.

But as they started to push it, the lizard raced out.

'Stop him!' Izzie shouted as it scuttled past her and through the bedroom door.

Eddie leapt at the lizard in the same way he'd tried to save a goal on the football pitch that afternoon. He hadn't managed to save the goal and he didn't manage to stop the lizard either – although it was very close. So close he felt its little claws tickle him as it ran over his hand.

He scrambled to his feet and bumped into Izzie. 'Ouch!' he cried.

Toby ran down the passageway after the lizard, dripping dollops of strawberry jam on the carpet as he did so. 'Here, lizardy wizardy!'

The lizard ran along the passageway towards the front door. Just at that moment it swung open.

'Stop it!' everyone screamed as the lizard got to the doorway.

And a huge hand reached down and scooped up the lizard.

CHAPTER 4

'It's okay, little one,' Dad's deep, kind voice said to the lizard cupped in his hands. 'You're safe here. No one's going to harm you.'

'Oh, you came back just in time!' Mum said, hurrying to the door.

'Don't frighten it now. Sudden movements and shouting will only panic it,' Dad said as he carried the lizard into the kitchen.

Everyone followed him. They all sat around the small rickety table – apart from Toby, who sat on the floor and played with the truck that he'd spotted underneath it.

Izzie and Eddie told their dad what had happened.

'He was almost forgotten. We couldn't leave him behind . . .' said Izzie.

'It's not a gecko, is it, Dad?' Eddie said. 'Geckos don't have claws, do they? They have sucker pads.'

His dad knew more about animals than anyone else Eddie could think of. But even his dad had never met anything quite like the lizard before.

'The leopard gecko does have claws but this isn't a gecko – although he is similar,'

Dad said. 'Perhaps he's a horned lizard.'

He opened his fingers a crack so he could take another look. The lizard's golden eyes blinked up at him.

'It's old. Five years at least,' Eddie said.

'That *is* old for a lizard in captivity,' Dad agreed.

'It doesn't even have a name – Miss Harper said we could give it one,' Izzie said.

'Has he had any food since he arrived? What does he usually eat?' Dad asked them.

'We've got some lizard pellets for him,' Izzie said. She went to get the food and Eddie went to fetch the lizard's tank. Dad put the lizard back inside and he immediately scuttled into the cave.

Izzie put a few lizard pellets on his food dish but the lizard didn't come out of the cave to eat them. 'He's a bit grumpy,' she said.

'Give him time,' Dad said, as Eddie and Izzie looked into the tank.

'I'm glad we brought him home,' said Eddie.

'Me too,' said Dad.

Then Izzie remembered what Mrs Winters had said. 'But what about the No Pet rule?'

'What No Pet rule?' Dad asked.

'That pets are not allowed at Willow View. But having a lizard's not like having a dog or a cat in the flat, is it?' said Eddie.

'But Mrs Winters said someone had to leave because they had a canary,' Izzie said.

Mum fetched the rent contract and turned the pages. 'Pets are strictly forbidden,' she read, and she bit her bottom lip. 'We don't want to get evicted.'

Dad squeezed Mum's hand. 'It'll be all right. We just have to make sure we keep him hidden.'

'At least he's only small,' said Eddie. 'And we've got lots of lizard pellets so we won't need to buy him any food.'

'And lizards don't usually do much,' said Izzie, 'so he's not likely to be noticed.'

CHAPTER 5

'How was the job centre?' Mum asked Dad a few days later, as she made him a cup of tea.

Every day it was open Dad went to the job centre to try to find a job. He also looked through the newspapers and on the internet at the library, but so far he hadn't had much luck. When Toby started at nursery next term, Mum was hoping to get a job, too.

Dad shook his head. 'I know there has to be a job somewhere out there for me. All I have to do is find it,' he said.

'And it's my *bathday*,' said Toby, coming out from under the table.

'Not yet,' Izzie told him. 'Six more big sleeps and then it's your *birthday*.'

'At least it's Friday today,' said Mum. 'So you know what we should do to celebrate?'

'Go on the roof?' Eddie grinned.

'With popcorn,' said Izzie.

'Yeeeees!' said Eddie.

They'd had to move to the flat when the lavender farm where Dad worked closed down and he'd lost his job. The flat was on the very top floor of the building, and was tiny and damp and rundown. The wallpaper had been up for so long it had turned brown and sometimes the water that came out of the taps was brown too. Their tower block was called Willow View, but there were no trees at all nearby and hardly any grass, just lots more grey concrete buildings.

But there was something *very* good and totally unexpected about their flat, that no one had mentioned to them . . .

One day, about two weeks after they'd moved in, Izzie and Eddie had noticed there was a door behind the peeling wallpaper. When they pulled the paper away and unbolted the door, they found a metal ladder that led onto the roof. The roof had a high wall all the way round it.

Dad checked to see if the roof was safe before they went out on it, but once he'd tested it, out they went. From that day on, the tower block roof became their very own large yard. It wasn't the same as living in one of the cottages on the farm like they used to, of course, but it was much better than having no garden at all. Mum and Dad were already trying to grow plants and vegetables on it and everyone liked being out there in the sun during the day, and sitting on it at night and looking up at the stars.

None of the other residents on the top floor came out onto the roof so they supposed they must be the only ones with a door.

Now Mum made a huge bowl of popcorn while Izzie and Toby collected up some cushions and blankets and an old deckchair for them to sit on.

Eddie went into the bedroom to get a jumper. The lizard was in its tank on top of the chest of drawers. Since they'd brought it home it had spent most of its time inside the cave, asleep. But then it *was* very old.

Eddie dropped a few more lizard pellets into its dish. It hadn't eaten many of them so far.

'I wonder how often he's been outside,' Dad said to Eddie.

'Not often enough, I'd say,' said Eddie. 'I bet he'd love being out on the roof.'

'Me too,' said Dad, and he picked up the tank and they took the lizard out with them.

They put the plastic tank next to the

blanket as Mum came out to join them with the popcorn.

The lizard poked its head out of the ornamental cave, went back in again, and then came out and looked through the clear plastic up at the sky. It was the most active they'd seen him since that first day when he'd run down the passageway.

'Here, poor lizardy wizardy,' Toby said, dropping a bit of popcorn into the lizard's tank.

The lizard raced back into his cave.

'No, Toby,' said Eddie. 'He won't like that.'

But Eddie was wrong. They all watched in

amazement as the lizard came out of the cave again and licked at the popcorn.

The lizard hadn't eaten many of the lizard pellets they'd put in his dish – maybe he wanted popcorn instead.

It wasn't dark yet, but Izzie could see

the white moon and the evening star above them.

The lizard looked up again at the sky, stood on his back legs and stretched out his front claws as far up the tank as he could get. He'd never done anything like that before!

'I think he wants to come out,' Izzie said. 'Can I hold him, Dad, if I'm very careful?'

'Only if he wants to be held. Put your hand in the tank. If he moves away, he's not ready. If he climbs into your hand, he is. Do it slowly, though – you don't want to frighten him. That's probably why he ran away before.'

Izzie nodded and put one of her hands into the tank and kept it very still and waited.

The lizard looked at Izzie's hand, and

then back up at the sky. Izzie held her breath as he edged closer, then closer still . . . until finally he crawled into her hand. Izzie lifted the lizard out of the tank and held him on her lap as the lizard looked up at the stars and the moon and made a strange, almost happy-sounding little snuffle.

CHAPTER 6

Mum was always trying to persuade Toby to eat anything other than just strawberry jam sandwiches, and she was trying again at breakfast a couple of days later.

'Eating the same food all the time isn't good for you,' Eddie told Toby.

'How about some spaghetti hoops?' said Mum.

'Or some baked beans?' said Eddie.

'Or an apple,' said Izzie.

Toby just shook his head at every suggestion they made.

'Just try a spoonful of cornflakes,' Mum said, pouring some into a bowl and adding milk. 'Just one spoonful won't hurt you.'

But Toby didn't want to eat the cornflakes. 'Milk make them slimy an' soggy,' he said, looking down at the bowl Mum had put in front of him.

'Then try some without any milk,' Mum said, tipping a few flakes from the packet into another bowl.

Dad came into the kitchen and, while Mum was making him coffee, Toby took the little bowl of cornflakes into the bedroom.

He came back a few minutes later. 'All gone,' he said.

'Oh good,' said Mum. 'I'm glad you liked them.'

'Lizard ate them.'

'What?'

Everyone hurried to the bedroom. There were just a few crumbs of cornflakes left in the lizard's tank.

'He couldn't have eaten them all, could he?' Izzie asked.

'Yes he did,' said Toby. 'He went *crunch munch crunch.*'

Izzie fetched the packet and put three more cornflakes on his food dish and the lizard picked them up in his claws and ate them one after the other, making tiny crunches as everyone watched him.

The lizard had quite liked the popcorn Toby had given him, but he *loved* the cornflakes.

'He's so cute,' Izzie laughed, as the lizard finished off the last one and looked up at her with its head tilted to one side. 'Can I give him some more?'

'Just a few, then,' Dad said. 'Remember, he's only little.'

'More cornflakes, little lizard?' Izzie said as she put two more on his dish.

 The lizard crunched them up and then made a growly sort of noise that sounded very much to both

Eddie and Izzie like, 'More.'

'That's it!' Eddie said.

'What is?'

'Miss Harper said we could name him. We should call him Cornflake.'

The lizard made a sound that was a bit like a burp and a bit like a bark and everyone laughed.

'Can I give Cornflake some more cornflakes, Dad?' Izzie asked.

But Dad shook his head. 'That's enough for now, although you could try him with some fruit later. Some lizards like little bits of apple and some like eggs – that's what they'd eat in the wild. I've heard lots of lizards like cat food – chicken rather than fish flavour, so we could try that. It's a shame your teacher didn't tell you if he ate meat or plants.'

'I don't think even Miss Harper would have guessed he'd like cornflakes,' said Eddie.

'He looks happier, Dad,' said Izzie. 'It's almost like Cornflake's smiling at us.'

And everyone agreed.

CHAPTER 7

The first thing Eddie did when he woke up the next morning was look over at Cornflake's tank.

'Oh no!' Eddie said.

Izzie opened her eyes. 'What's wrong?'

'Cornflake's missing.'

Izzie threw back the bed covers and almost jumped out of bed, but stopped herself just in time. She got out carefully instead, because she didn't want to accidentally step on Cornflake if he was on the carpet.

'You check in here, I'll check the rest of the flat,' Eddie said, as he headed out of the room.

Toby didn't wake up. When Toby was asleep nothing could wake him until he was ready.

Dad was in the bathroom having a shower before his meeting at the job centre.

'Everything all right?' Mum asked sleepily from under the covers of the sofa bed.

'No – Cornflake's escaped from his tank.'

Mum immediately got up to help look for him too.

When Eddie went into the kitchen he

 found a cereal packet on the floor and picked it up.

'He's not in the bedroom,' Izzie said, coming to join him. She looked at the packet he was holding. 'You should be looking for Cornflake not eating breakfast.'

'I'm not eating breakfast. This was lying on the floor and I picked it up. It's really heavy, though . . .'

He looked down at the open packet – there were no cornflakes in there, but there was a cornflake-orange-coloured lizard with fiery eyes and a very round stomach looking back at him!

'I've found Cornflake!'

Izzie stared into the box too. 'He looks a bit bigger than last night,' she said.

When Izzie lifted Cornflake out of the box she realised he was almost half as big again as he'd been when they'd brought him home.

Dad came into the kitchen and smiled when he saw them.

'What are those bumps on his shoulders, Dad?' asked Izzie. He definitely hadn't had bumps there before.

'He's got small points along his back too,' Eddie said. 'He didn't have those yesterday, did he? I'm sure we'd have noticed.'

'He's not sick is he, Dad?' Izzie said. She really didn't want him to be. 'It's not because he ate too many cornflakes, is it?'

'He doesn't look like he's sick,' Dad said.

'Although he's probably got a tummy-ache from being so greedy. Eating all those cornflakes can't have been good for him. I'll ask at the pet shop on the way home if they know what could be wrong with him. You two could look on the library computer and see what you can find out. In the meantime, keep an eye on him and get him some cat food to try instead.'

Dad hurried off to the job centre as Izzie took Cornflake back to his tank. He could barely fit in the ornamental cave now.

'It can't be good for him to just eat cornflakes, even if he does like them very much,' Eddie said, as he put a tray over the top of Cornflake's tank to stop him getting out again.

'He should eat san'wicks instead,' Toby said, yawning from his bed.

'He's going to try cat food,' Izzie told him.

'Lizardy's not a cat,' Toby said.

'Dad thinks he might like it,' said Eddie.

'We need some more teabags while you're out shopping,' Mum said. 'Oh, and bread and strawberry jam and more cornflakes, of course, and some small candles.'

'For my *bathday* cake.' Toby smiled.

CHAPTER 8

Eddie and Izzie were standing by the pet food aisle in the supermarket trying to decide which brand of cat food Cornflake might like best when Izzie felt someone watching her. She turned round, but she couldn't see anyone looking at them.

'I wonder why Dad thinks cat food would be better for him than dog food,' Eddie said, picking up a tin and reading the ingredients on the back.

Izzie tried to focus on them too, but soon had the same strange feeling of someone watching her again. She could almost feel eyes staring at her. She was even more sure when she caught a glimpse of a familiar pink shoe at the end of the aisle, out of the corner of her eye.

Eddie picked up more tins. 'Cats are very picky eaters so I guess they probably know what's good for them . . .'

Izzie tiptoed up the aisle to the end.

'Hello, Mrs Winters,' Izzie said, coming up behind her.

Mrs Winters almost jumped out of her skin. 'Oh my,' she said, as Eddie came to join them too. 'What a surprise! Fancy finding you two here by the pet food aisle of all places. Are you getting a cat? Or maybe you already have one? I can't think why else you'd be here.' Her beady eyes looked sharply from one of them to the other.

Eddie shook his head but looked guilty.

'Just seeing what's here,' Izzie said.

'Indeed,' said Mrs Winters, raising an eyebrow. She didn't sound like she believed Izzie one little bit.

'Well, we'd better get on,' Izzie said, pulling Eddie away to the bakery aisle and dropping a loaf into their basket. They waited until Mrs Winters had gone and then they doubled back, determined to get Cornflake some cat food.

This time Eddie kept a lookout while Izzie picked up two tins of chicken with extra jelly. She put them into the basket to join the bread, teabags and birthday cake candles.

'Can you see her?' she asked him.

'Nope.'

Eddie kept looking around to see if he could spot Mrs Winters as they hurried

to the checkout with their basket.

'Any sign of her?' Izzie asked him as she unloaded the items and paid for them.

'None.'

Izzie packed their bag, and then they hurried out of the shop and ran all the way back to Willow View without visiting the library.

'You were very quick,' Mum said, when they came bursting back in through the front door.

'Mrs Winters thinks we've got a cat,' Eddie said.

'She was spying on us at the pet food aisle,' said Izzie.

'I'm sure there's nothing to worry about,' said Mum.

But Eddie and Izzie weren't so sure.

'What about the No Pets rule? She's such a busybody,' Izzie said.

'She's spiteful and nasty,' said Eddie.

'She's not nasty,' Mum said. 'I think she's just lonely.'

Toby came in, pulling his red truck on a string with Cornflake sitting on the back of it. The lizard looked so funny that Izzie laughed and laughed, and then she laughed

even more when Cornflake made a funny
little sound as if he was laughing too.

'I told you not to touch Cornflake's tank,
Toby,' Mum said, although she was smiling.

'Lizardy wizardy wanted to go for a ride,'
Toby said.

'His name's Cornflake now,' said Eddie.

'Can Cornflake have a strawberry jam
san-wick?' Toby asked.

'You can have a sandwich,' Mum said,
getting out the strawberry jam. 'Cornflake's
going to try some cat food.'

Eddie opened the pouch and put a bit of
the chicken in jelly on a saucer.

'Here you are, Cornflake.'

Cornflake looked at the saucer of food
and then up at Eddie.

'Go on,' Eddie said, pointing at it.

Cornflake's black tongue came out and he licked at it a little bit and then took a few mouthfuls.

'He's not wolfing it down like he does the cornflakes,' Izzie said.

'Lizardy don't like it,' said Toby.

'No, but at least he's trying it,' said Mum. 'You could try something too.'

'Okay,' Toby said. 'I'll try, like Cornflake. But not cat food.'

'No.' Mum smiled. 'Why don't you try a slice of banana?'

Toby chewed the banana very slowly and didn't look like he was enjoying it much, but at least he'd tried it and that made Mum happy.

Cornflake climbed back into Toby's truck with most of the cat food left untouched on the plate.

'He's probably still full from all the cornflakes he ate this morning,' Izzie said.

Eddie nodded. 'He did eat a lot of them.

Do you think those lumps on his shoulders look bigger?'

'The spikes down his back are almost triangle-shaped now, and he does seem to have grown a lot,' Izzie said. 'He's almost filling the back of Toby's truck.'

Mum had just put the saucer of cat food in the fridge when the doorbell rang and made Izzie jump. The ringing was followed by an impatient knocking.

'Who on earth can that be?' Mum said.

CHAPTER 9

'*Brmm brmm*,' said Toby as he pulled the truck with Cornflake on it down the passage. Cornflake had been in the back of the truck for so long now he was almost the same colour red as it.

Toby was not supposed to open the front door unless someone else was with him. But he opened it anyway.

'Hello,' he said, as Izzie, Eddie and Mum ran towards the door.

'Mrs Winters, what a lovely surprise,' Mum said, her voice much higher than usual.

'I demand that you let me come in,' Mrs Winters said.

She brushed past Toby, not noticing Cornflake in the truck.

'How about a cup of tea, Mrs Winters?' Mum asked, quickly following her. 'You must be thirsty after all that shopping.'

'No, thank you,' Mrs Winters said, brushing past Toby once again and heading into the children's bedroom where Eddie was.

'It's in here, isn't it?' she said.

'What is?' asked Eddie.

'The cat you're trying to keep hidden. I

know it is. I was so sure . . .' But she sounded
a bit doubtful now. She saw Cornflake's
tank, but of course it was empty.

'Not a kitty cat – it's Cornflake,' Toby said.

Eddie gulped and Izzie's mouth fell open.
Now Mrs Winters would know for certain
that they did have a pet.

But Mrs Winters didn't pay any attention
to Toby.

The front door opened again.

'Hello, Mrs Winters,' Dad said. 'It's nice
to see you.'

'I've got to be getting on,' she said.

'Stay for my *bathday*,' said Toby, smiling
his most winning smile.

But Mrs Winters had already bustled her
way out of the flat.

'Phew!' said Eddie.

'That was close,' said Izzie. 'I almost told her to mind her own business.'

'I'm glad you didn't,' Mum said. 'I think she's such a sad lady.'

'Where's Cornflake?' Dad asked.

'Here,' said Toby, pointing at the large red bulge in the back of his truck. 'He's sleeping.'

'I think he's grown even bigger than when I left this morning,' Dad said, looking puzzled. He crouched down to get a closer look. 'I asked at the pet shop but their lizard specialist didn't know what could be wrong with him.'

'He's not really, really sick, is he?' Izzie asked. She had a nasty, sinking feeling.

'Miss Harper did tell us he was very old and he might not live much longer.' She really didn't want Cornflake to die, especially now they'd become friends.

'I don't see how he can be. But I've never heard of a lizard growing this fast. He doesn't even look much like a lizard any more,' Dad said.

'He's almost the size of a small kitten,' said Mum.

Cornflake opened his eyes and gave a big yawn.

'Even those nodules on his shoulders have grown,' Dad said as he stood up.

Cornflake stood up too and stretched.

'Oh,' Izzie gasped as the nodules on Cornflake's back suddenly opened. 'Is

Cornflake okay? What's happening to him?'

'He *is* sick,' Eddie said.

But Cornflake wasn't sick. They all watched in amazement as tiny wings uncurled themselves from where the nodules had been.

'I don't understand,' said Izzie.

'Me neither,' Mum said. 'What's going on?'

But Dad could only shake his head. 'I don't know.'

Cornflake got down from the back of the truck and ran along the passage and back again, making little jumping movements every now and again as his new wings flapped up and down.

'It's almost like he's trying to get himself off the ground,' Izzie said.

'He's trying to fly,' said Eddie.

Eddie and Izzie looked at each other and suddenly both of them grinned.

'What do you call a flying lizard?' Eddie said.

'A dragon!' replied Izzie.

CHAPTER 10

'Those spines along his back and tail must be for flight stabilising,' Eddie said, as they watched Cornflake trying to take off.

But hard as he tried, Cornflake wasn't able to fly.

'He'll exhaust himself,' Mum said, as the little dragon ran up and down the passage, making angry, frustrated squawks.

He didn't even stop when there was a rattling at the letterbox and Mrs Winters's beady eyes looked through it. 'That sounds just like a parrot. Have you got a bird in there?'

'Oh no, Mrs Winters,' Izzie said, standing in front of the letterbox as Cornflake bumped into the wall and lay down. 'I'm sorry we were playing so noisily.'

'Lizardy try fly,' said Toby.

But Mrs Winters ignored him as usual.

'You can't fool me,' she said. 'I know something's going on.' And she let the letterbox drop with a bang.

As soon as she did, Cornflake jumped up off the floor and headed to the bedroom. Izzie, Eddie and Toby followed him.

They were just in time to see the small dragon climb onto Toby's bed and launch himself off it with his little wings flapping desperately – only to land with a thump on the floor.

'I wish we could help him somehow,' Izzie said.

But none of them knew how to fly either.

For the rest of the day, with only a few short breaks to drink some water and eat a cornflake or two, the little dragon kept on practising.

'The problem is his wings are too small and his body's too big,' Eddie said.

'No, I think the real problem is he can't get a long enough run-up,' said Izzie. 'There's just not enough space in our flat for

Cornflake to launch himself properly.'

'I've got an idea of how we can help him,' Dad said. 'He'll get more of a run-up if we take him up to the roof.'

Once it was getting dark, they went out onto the flat roof.

Cornflake ran across it and managed for a moment to fly.

He was so excited he squealed as his wings flapped like mad before letting him down.

Cornflake ran across the roof again, and this time he was able to stay in the air for ten whole seconds.

'Yeah, Cornflake!' Izzie cheered.

'Go, dragon!' shouted Eddie.

'Stop all that noise!' Mrs Winters shouted up to them through the top of her bathroom window.

CHAPTER 11

'Cornflake is very rare,' Dad explained to the children the next day. 'He might be the only dragon in the world, in fact.'

'And that means,' said Mum, 'that it's even more important we keep him a secret.'

'Why?' Toby asked.

'A dragon would be worth a lot of money to some people,' Dad said.

'They wouldn't try to steal him from us, would they?' Izzie said feeling very worried. She really didn't want Cornflake to be taken away.

'Not if they don't know about him,' said Mum.

'We'll be extra careful,' Izzie said and Eddie nodded.

'Don't want someone else to have lizardy wizardy,' said Toby.

'Why don't you see if you can find anything else out about dragons from the library?' Dad said to Eddie and Izzie. 'Now we know what he is, there might be some information on dragons that could be useful.'

Izzie frowned. 'I didn't ever think dragons could be real,' she said. 'Not really real.'

'Me neither,' said Eddie. 'Come on, let's see what we can find out.'

'Have you got any books on dragons?' Izzie asked the librarian.

'Lots,' he told her. 'And there'll be more information on the internet too.'

They looked through all the dragon books

but they weren't much practical help, and none of the dragons in them ate cornflakes. At the end of the last book, there was a message that said:

If you believe you may have seen a dragon,
or any other unusual animal,
please contact us.

It gave a phone number to ring.

Eddie wrote down the number on a scrap of paper and then they sat down at the library's computer.

They typed all sorts of questions into the search engine. They asked what dragons liked to eat, how big they grew, how long they lived, how far they flew and how many dragons there were in the world. But the computer didn't seem to know the answer to any of the questions. Most of the time it just said:

Dragons are mythical creatures.

Suddenly the screen flickered and a messaged flashed up:

Dragon sightings should always be reported.

The message gave a telephone number.

'That's the same number that was in the book,' said Eddie.

'Do you think we should call it?' Izzie said. 'There's just a number – no name.'

'What if it belongs to someone who wants

to harm Cornflake?' said Eddie. 'I think we need to be very careful.'

Izzie and Eddie came back to find Toby and Cornflake sitting on the lounge floor in front of the sofa with the TV on.

Eddie grinned when he saw them. 'I don't believe it.'

Cornflake stared at the screen intently, and every now and then he blinked.

'Shhh,' Toby said, and he put his finger to his mouth as Izzie and Eddie went to join them on the floor.

The show was called *Dragon Days* and it was one of Toby's favourite cartoons. The dragons in it looked a little bit like Cornflake but they were definitely not real. Unlike him they could talk and wore clothes and lived in a dragon house in Dragon Town.

Cornflake didn't stop watching the programme until the credits came up and then he gave a little squawk of protest, as if he was cross that the show was over.

'He really did seem to be watching it,' Izzie said, 'but he couldn't have been, not really . . . Could he? Dragons don't watch TV.'

'He wants a dragon friend,' Toby said.

'He'd probably like one,' Eddie agreed.

'At least he's got us,' said Izzie.

Cornflake flapped his wings to fly up onto the windowsill and stared out at the sky.

That night, very late, Izzie and Eddie were woken by a beautiful but also sad and strange sound. It was coming from Cornflake, who was sitting and swaying on the windowsill and looking out into the darkness.

'What's he doing?' Izzie asked.

'He's singing,' said Eddie.

The little dragon's song went on and on until a cloud shifted and the moon was hidden. Then he hopped off the windowsill and went to sleep at the bottom of Toby's bed.

CHAPTER 12

Toby woke very early on the morning of his birthday. So early, in fact, that everyone else was still fast asleep.

Cornflake was snuggled up in the corner of the room with his head resting on a stuffed yellow teddy bear, so his head was now yellow too. No one would have guessed he was the library lizard any more. He was the size of a small cat, and his wings and the spikes along his back and tail were now clear to see.

'Happy *bathday* to me, happy *bathday* to me,' Toby sang to himself as soon as he woke up.

Cornflake had Toby's old highchair to sit on at the breakfast table. He looked at the cornflake packet and his little tongue went in and out. He looked up at Mum and she poured some into his dish.

'Cornflakes for me too,' said Toby. 'With strawberries, please.'

Mum poured him a bowl as well.

'Cornflakes crunchy, make you big and grow wings,' Toby said, as Izzie and Eddie came into the kitchen.

'Sorry, Toby, but you won't grow wings however many cornflakes you eat,' Izzie told him.

Toby looked sad and Eddie added gently, 'None of us will.'

'Just Cornflake?' Toby said, looking down at his bowl.

'Yes,' Eddie replied.

'Because he's a dragon?'

'Yes. But cornflakes are still nice to eat.'

Toby's favourite present was a green and yellow ride-on tractor with a trailer on the back of it from the second-hand shop.

Cornflake pounced on the gold-coloured wrapping paper as soon as Toby pulled it off and dropped it on the floor. He landed with a crash, and tore at the paper with his teeth, ripping it to shreds.

Mrs Winters banged on the wall to tell them to stop being so noisy.

'I wish she'd stop doing that,' huffed Izzie.

'She probably just wishes she could be part of Toby's birthday too,' Mum said. 'Don't feel too cross with her.'

'What's Cornflake doing that for?' asked Izzie.

'Maybe he thinks the paper is his prey,' Dad said, as the little dragon shook the paper vigorously.

'Weird, Cornflake,' Eddie told the little dragon. 'Very weird.'

'Get on, Cornflake,' Toby said, and Cornflake dropped the wrapping paper and hopped into the trailer and made a squawking noise.

At teatime, Toby got the strawberry jam cake he wanted and Mum put three candles on it.

Cornflake watched intently as she lit each one with a match. Then he opened his mouth and made a rumble deep in his throat.

Bathday song,' said Toby, his eyes shining. 'Sing me the *bathday* song now.'

And Izzie and Eddie and Mum and Dad did.

Cornflake blinked twice as Toby blew out the candles at the end of the song. He looked over at Mum, who was still holding the matches, and made a cawing sort of noise.

'Light them again for him,' said Eddie. He was sure that was what Cornflake wanted her to do.

Mum lit the three candles, but as Toby took a deep breath to blow them out again Cornflake opened his mouth very wide and then he jumped on top of the cake to get closer to the flames.

'No, Cornflake!' Izzie cried, as he sank into the icing. She scooped him up.

'He really does like those candles.' Eddie

grinned. 'Most animals are instinctively afraid of fire and run away from it. But not our Cornflake.'

After they'd eaten their cake, Toby carefully cut off a large slice from the end of the birthday cake that wasn't too squashed and put it on a small plate.

'Who's that for?' Eddie asked him.

'Mrs Winters,' Toby told him.

'You want to give some of your birthday cake to Mrs Winters?' Izzie asked Toby. Mrs Winters hadn't been very nice recently and she'd been banging on the wall only that morning.

Toby solemnly nodded. 'Mum said she want to be part of my *bathday*. Now she can be.'

Izzie looked at Mum, and Mum shook her head and smiled.

Toby held the slice of cake on the plate out in front of him as he made his way next door, followed by Eddie and Izzie, Mum and Dad.

Eddie pressed the doorbell and Toby knocked on the door with his foot.

'Mrs Winters, you in?' he shouted.

Mrs Winters opened the door.

'*Bath-day* cake,' Toby said, holding out the plate to Mrs Winters.

Mrs Winters stared down at the plate. 'For me? You brought a slice of your birthday cake for me?'

Toby nodded. 'Strawberry, mmmm.'

Mrs Winters looked very surprised but

she took the cake anyway. 'Thank you so much,' she said.

'That was a very nice thought,' Mum said to Toby as they headed back along the corridor to their own flat. 'I think she was pleased.'

But as they reached their front door they smelled smoke.

'Stay back!' Dad shouted. He carefully opened the door as the rest of them crowded round behind him.

Cornflake was in the passage. His mouth was open really wide and he was making a coughing sound. The smoke was coming out of his mouth!

'What's he doing?' said Mum.

'He's a dragon,' said Eddie.

'Yes!' said Izzie. 'He's trying to breathe fire!'

As she said this, a tiny burst of flames came shooting out of Cornflake's mouth, leaving a small brown scorch mark on the wallpaper.

Cornflake opened his mouth really *really* wide, ready to try again.

'No!' Mum shouted. 'No flames!'

Cornflake looked at her with his head tilted to one side, as if he were listening to her. Then he gave a little flame cough.

'NO!' Mum shouted very loudly this time.

Cornflake looked like he understood because he put his head down as if he'd been naughty, and stopped trying to cough up flames.

'You've made him sad, Mum,' Eddie said.

'Better sad than burnt up,' said Mum.

CHAPTER 13

Over the next two weeks Izzie and Eddie found out that having even a smallish dragon living in their tiny flat could be very awkward. And no one knew how big he'd eventually grow.

Cornflake was only allowed to try breathing fire when he was outside on the roof. But even though Cornflake did his best not to, sometimes he couldn't help himself. Usually he produced smoke, and when he did breathe fire, the flames he produced weren't strong enough for anything to catch light, but a few things got singed. Mum and Dad were very worried.

Dad installed an extra smoke alarm so at least they'd be warned in time if Cornflake started a fire by mistake. But now Mrs Winters was forever banging on the wall and complaining about the noise of the alarm.

'It must be faulty,' she said. 'No one can burn toast that often!'

There were soon lots of scorch marks on the wallpaper, and the furniture wasn't looking much better either.

'We'll have to replace all the damaged things,' Mum said.

There were two weeks left of the school holidays. Eddie and Izzie were off to get food again – Cornflake was eating more and more. A packet of cornflakes only lasted a few days and now he'd started on the Rice Krispies and Coco-pops too.

'Strawberry jam!' Toby called after Eddie and Izzie as they headed out.

In the lift they overheard some of the people from other flats talking about a strange man they'd met on the estate.

'He kept asking me all sorts of odd

questions and staring at me from behind those green glasses . . .'

'He asked us too – nosy-parker sort of chap, if you ask me. Wanted to know if we'd seen any unusual animals. I told him we don't see any *usual* animals around let alone *unusual* ones.'

Eddie and Izzie gave each other a look. They'd seen a very unusual animal but they wouldn't be telling the nosy-parker man about it.

'I thought it was very strange,' the first person said.

'Me too,' said another.

Eddie and Izzie were on their way back to the flat with the shopping when a bald man with green glasses stopped the lift just as the doors were about to close. Izzie and Eddie pressed themselves against the very back of the lift as he stepped inside.

'You two look like observant children,' the man said. 'Perhaps you can help me.'

Eddie and Izzie looked at each other. This must be the nosy parker.

'Um, not really,' Eddie said, and Izzie shook her head.

'Oh, come now. You'd notice if there was something here that shouldn't be,' the man said. 'Something out of the ordinary . . . an unusual creature, perhaps?' He peered sharply from Izzie to Eddie and back again, as if he were trying to catch them out.

'Not us,' said Izzie.

'But – ' the man started to say when the lift stopped again and the door squealed and groaned its way open.

Mr Banton, the Willow View window cleaner, came in holding a bucket of soapy water and a brush. Even though it wasn't their floor, Izzie and Eddie quickly got out of the lift before the nosy parker asked them any more questions.

The last thing Izzie saw as the door squealed closed was the nosy parker still looking at them.

'I don't like him,' said Izzie as they headed up the stairs.

'Me neither,' said Eddie. 'What's he

doing here and why is he asking all those questions?'

They were almost home when Izzie grabbed Eddie's arm. 'Look!'

She pointed down to the ground. The nosy parker was standing opposite their building, looking through a pair of binoculars to the top of the Willow View tower block.

'He's looking up at the roof,' Eddie said, and then he and Izzie panicked because their roof garden was where Cornflake liked to spend a lot of his time these days. Was he up there now?

'Hurry!'

They had to make sure the nosy parker didn't see him.

'Izzie? Eddie? Come here quickly!' Mum called, as they went in. Her voice sounded strange – sort of squeaky.

Izzie and Eddie ran into the lounge. They were both relieved to see that Cornflake was in there, and not on the roof after all.

'What's he doing?'

'Copying me.'

Mum was doing her Tai Chi exercises to some tinkling music on a TV programme. As she made the slow, flowing movements, Cornflake was doing his best to do the same.

'I didn't dare sit down in case he stopped before you saw him,' Mum said out of the corner of her mouth as she lifted and raised her arms, and Cornflake lifted and raised his wings.

Eddie and Izzie watched him in amazement.

A few minutes later the music stopped and so did Mum and Cornflake.

The little dragon looked at the cornflake packet poking out of the shopping bag and squawked.

Toby woke up from his nap, turned the TV to his channel and started dancing along to one of his shows.

'Arms up high to touch the sky,
Then down low, to and fro . . .'

'Come on, Cornflake,' he shouted, and Cornflake joined him.

Eddie and Izzie looked at each other. Toby and Cornflake were dancing together!

Eddie and Izzie laughed and then joined in. Toby got so excited he started jumping up and down.

Cornflake looked from one child to another and then he flapped his wings and bounced up and down too, but he had wings so he managed to bounce a lot higher – all the way up to the ceiling, where he gave a squawk as he bumped his head.

'Oh no!' said Mum as she looked up.

Cornflake didn't seem to have really hurt himself but he'd definitely hurt the ceiling. It had a big dent in it and some of the paint and plaster came floating down.

'More dragon damage!' she said and she sounded really cross and looked a bit desperate as she ran her hands through her hair. 'He's spoiling everything.'

Cornflake tried not to go so high the next time, but it was really hard when he was

so springy and had wings that helped him
go up very far.

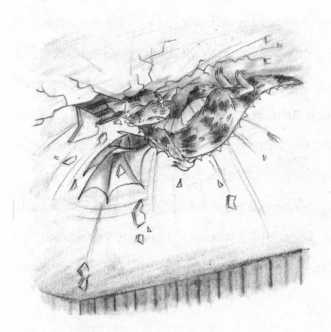

Later that night, Eddie and Izzie overheard Mum and Dad's muffled voices talking softly in the lounge.

'He could grow much bigger and he's already damaging things . . .'

'He can't stay in this tiny flat for ever . . . But it's not like he can go back to school. He's not a library lizard any more, and he can't even fit in his tank now.'

'If only we knew what we should do for the best . . .'

Cornflake gave a loud sigh, and Eddie and Izzie looked over at him and realised that the little dragon had been listening too.

CHAPTER 14

Dad was whistling when he came home from the job centre the next day. 'Guess what?' he said.

'What?' said Eddie.

'I've got a job interview tomorrow,' Dad said. 'It's as a caretaker. I applied for it weeks ago and had just about given up on it but they contacted the job centre and said they'd like to see me. It comes with a little house! If I get it, we'll be able to move out of here and we'll be in the country and have a garden again.'

A house in the country with a garden sounded perfect. And although no one said it, it might mean they'd be able to keep Cornflake.

Dad was so happy about the interview for the caretaker's job that he went around the house singing.

'I'm sure this is the one,' he said, giving Mum a kiss and ruffling Toby's hair.

'They're bound to give it to you once they meet you,' Eddie said. Anyone who got to know his dad would like him.

Dad was still cheery when he left the next

morning. 'See you later,' Dad said, as he went whistling out of the door.

'Mum?' Izzie said, as she washed the breakfast things.

'Yes?'

'We'll be okay if Dad doesn't get this job, won't we?'

'Of course we will,' Mum said, although she didn't sound like she totally meant it.

'Only, where will we live if we can't pay the rent? And what about Cornflake?'

Ever since she'd heard Mum and Dad talking, she'd been worrying about what would happen to Cornflake. If Dad got the job, all their problems would be solved. But if he didn't . . .

'He'll get another job soon,' Eddie said,

coming into the kitchen. 'I bet he gets this one today.'

Izzie nodded but she was still worried. Dad had been for interviews before and he hadn't got those jobs.

She heard splashing and a lot of laughter coming from the bathroom.

'What's that?'

Eddie, Izzie and Mum hurried out of the kitchen to see what was going on.

'Cornflake wanted bath,' Toby said, pointing at the little dragon splashing about in the water. He'd only been in the bath for a few seconds but already there was water all over the floor. 'He turned taps on.'

'Toby, he could have drowned!' Izzie said, quickly turning the taps off. But the truth was, Cornflake seemed to be quite at home in the water.

The people in the flat below them hadn't complained about the fire alarm going off, but they came rushing up the stairs and banged on the door when water dripped through their ceiling.

'I'm sorry! I'm sorry!' Mum said. 'The bath overflowed.'

'It was my fault,' Toby told them. He looked so sad that they said it was all right, but they asked Mum to make sure it didn't happen again.

Instead, that evening when it was time for Toby's bath, Cornflake flapped his way into the shallow water with him and his yellow ducks, and the next morning Dad found he had a small dragon with him in the shower.

'Morning, Cornflake,' he said, as Cornflake stretched up his chin so his neck got water on it too.

Dad had been happy ever since he got back from the interview and all the family were sure he was likely to get the job because the interview had gone so well.

'Do most reptiles like water, Dad?' Eddie asked him. 'Or is Cornflake unique?'

'Some do and some don't,' Dad said. 'But I think its still safe to say that Cornflake is unique.'

A few moments later the job centre phoned and Izzie watched as her dad's face went from happy to sad and then sadder still.

'It's okay . . . No, I do understand . . . There are lots of good candidates . . . Maybe next time . . . Yes, thanks. Goodbye.'

'Sorry, Dad,' said Izzie, as he put the phone down.

'They're so stupid not giving the job to you,' said Eddie.

'At least you've had an interview,' Mum said. 'Something else will come along, I'm sure of it.'

Dad shook his head. 'There are so many people looking for work. It's hard to compete.'

He sat and then lay down on the sofa.

'I hate Dad looking so sad,' Izzie whispered to Eddie as Toby crawled under his bed to see what he could find there.

'Me too,' Eddie whispered back. 'I wish there was something we could do to cheer him up.'

'Mum, have you seen Corn—' Izzie started to say.

Mum put her finger to her lips and nodded at the sofa.

Dad was lying stretched out on it, fast asleep and Cornflake was lying stretched out on Dad's chest, fast asleep too.

'They look very comfy.' Izzie grinned, and Mum squeezed her hand.

As they watched, Cornflake made a happy, sleepy sort of snuffle and rolled over onto his back with his legs in the air. A tear rolled down Izzie's face because she felt so sad. Cornflake was part of their family now and this was his home. But how were they going to be able to keep him?

'Cornflake's smiling,' Eddie said, coming into the room to join them.

'I wonder what he's dreaming about,' said Izzie.

They knew so little about the dragon –

not where he came from or if he had parents who were still alive, or how he'd ended up as a school pet.

Izzie bit her bottom lip. 'What will happen to Cornflake now?' she asked.

'We'll find a way,' said Mum. 'Don't worry.'

But that night Cornflake helped himself to a midnight feast while everyone else was asleep. He ate all the cornflakes and then he opened the fridge to see what was inside and left the door open.

'All the food's ruined,' Mum said the next morning. 'He's eating us out of house and home. I only went shopping yesterday and now it's all gone.' And she burst into tears because there just wasn't enough money to waste food. 'I don't know how we can afford to keep feeding him!'

Cornflake managed to look both guilty and sad at the same time.

CHAPTER 15

After breakfast there was only one place Cornflake wanted to be. He would flap his way to the door that led to the roof and give a loud squawk.

The next day, Cornflake was especially keen to get outside.

'One minute!' Izzie called as she tried to finish her breakfast as quickly as she could.

Cornflake squawked again – louder this time.

'Okay, okay,' Eddie said, and he took his half-eaten toast with him as he went to open the door where Cornflake was waiting. 'What's the rush?'

Once the door was unlocked, Cornflake sped up the ladder. Eddie followed him and Izzie came to join them. They never let Cornflake or Toby up onto the roof by themselves.

Eddie breathed in the fresh rooftop air. It was stuffy in the flat and the weather had turned very hot and humid. He didn't blame Cornflake for wanting to spend all day up here. Not one little bit. When they'd first seen the nosy parker, they'd been a bit worried about letting Cornflake go on the roof during the day. But they were less worried now – it had been a few days since anyone had seen him.

Cornflake scuttled to the spot that got the most morning sun and lay down on his back, his little round tummy facing upwards.

'Play hide and seek,' Toby said, when he came up to join them ten minutes later. It was Toby's current favourite game.

'I don't think Cornflake wants to play – he's sunbathing,' Izzie said.

But at that moment Cornflake's golden eyes opened and he jumped up, ran over to the largest of the plant pots, hid behind it and peeped out at Toby.

Toby grinned with delight, put his hands

122

over his eyes and started counting. 'Seven, two, one, nine, eight . . .'

Izzie and Eddie ran to find hiding places on the roof too. There weren't very many – apart from behind plant pots!

'Never thought we'd be playing hide and seek with a dragon,' Eddie said as Toby found him and it was his turn to find the others. He had to pretend not to find them too quickly.

When Mum came out to play too, Cornflake ran about the roof squawking. They all knew he was just excited, and didn't mean to knock over Mum's very best plant pot. It was an accident.

'Nooooooo!' Mum cried, as it toppled over and smashed into hundreds of pieces. 'Gran gave that to me!'

'A person can't think with all that racket going on up there!' Mrs Winters shouted through the top of her bathroom window. But fortunately she couldn't see what was going on and mistakenly thought the squawking was Toby having a temper tantrum.

'You'll do yourself a mischief with all that screaming,' Mrs Winters told a confused Toby when she saw him in the lift with Eddie and Izzie later.

But Eddie and Izzie were more interested in something else. As they were leaving the lift, they saw the nosy parker again.

'Come on, Toby,' Izzie said, taking her borther's hand as they hurried off in the opposite direction before the man could speak to them.

'Why are we running?' Toby complained.

'So we get to the shops quicker and get Cornflake some more cornflakes,' Izzie said.

Eddie looked behind him. The man had gone, so they slowed down.

'That's the third packet of cornflakes this week,' the shop assistant said. 'You must really like cornflakes at your house.'

'We do,' Toby told her.

In the evening, Mum made a huge bowl of popcorn and they took it out onto the roof as usual. It was the last Friday evening before Eddie and Izzie had to go back to school.

'We can't take him back there,' Eddie said desperately as he looked at Cornflake.

'Not now. He's nothing like the lizard we brought home.'

'But we can't keep him here either,' Mum said. 'There must be somewhere else he could go.'

'Not a zoo,' said Eddie as Cornflake stared up at him. 'He'd be stuck in a cage.'

'We have to do *something*,' Dad said. 'It's only a matter of time before he's spotted.'

The thought of not having Cornflake living with them was awful. He'd become such a big part of their family. It would feel all wrong without him there. Each mealtime he munched through his food while everyone else ate theirs. The bathroom door had to be firmly closed if you didn't want a little dragon in the shower with you these days.

And the children had enjoyed one of the best school holidays ever because they'd had Cornflake to play with.

Izzie brushed away a tear.

Cornflake looked from Eddie to Izzie and blinked. Then he looked at Mum and Dad and Toby. He gave a mournful cry, and the next moment he climbed up the wall surrounding the roof garden, peered downwards, and flew off into the sky.

CHAPTER 16

'No!' Izzie cried out.

It had been so quick, so unexpected. He'd gone before they could stop him, before they'd even really realised what was happening.

'Come back!' Eddie shouted.

But the little dragon didn't return.

'Lizardy wizardy!' screamed Toby.

'Cornflake!' Izzie yelled as loudly as she could.

But it was too late – he'd gone.

Izzie ran down the ladder back into the flat and out of the front door with Eddie and Dad right behind her. 'We have to follow him.'

'Me too!' shouted Toby, running after them, but Mum stopped him.

'No, Toby,' she said. 'You and I will wait for Cornflake on the roof in case he comes back.'

Toby shook his head as tears ran down his face. 'I don't want Cornflake to go away.'

'None of us do. Here, you shake his box of cornflakes. You know how he loves those. He'll be back. He probably just wanted to have a little look around, see what was out there.'

Toby wiped his tears away with his hand, took the box and shook it as they headed back out to the roof.

Izzie pressed the lift button and then pressed it again and again. 'Why does it always have to be so slow?' She pulled open the door to the stairs.

'Izzie, it's here,' Dad said, and she ran back and got in the lift too.

The lift never went fast but that night it seemed to creak its way down the lift shaft slower than a snail.

Eddie bit his bottom lip and Dad sighed.

Izzie couldn't bear it. 'He could be miles away by now,' she said.

'He's not used to flying far,' Dad said, but that only made it worse.

'What if he falls . . .?' said Izzie.

'He's never been out alone before. He won't know the way home.'

'He'll be lost and alone . . .'

'What if someone finds him?'

'They'll put him in a zoo or experiment on him or worse . . .' Izzie felt like she couldn't breathe. 'What if the nosy parker gets him?' Tears welled up in her eyes.

'Tears later,' Dad said. 'Now you need clear eyes so you can look for him.'

Izzie nodded and wiped away her tears.

'You look to the left, Eddie. Izzie, you look to the right,' Dad told them, as they headed down the street. 'And I'll look straight ahead. But try to keep together.'

The sudden appearance of the nosy parker in front of them made them all jump. 'Looking for someone . . . or something?' he said.

There wasn't time to reply. They had to find Cornflake.

'What's he doing here?' hissed Izzie as they hurried on.

'You don't think he's following us, do you, Dad?' Eddie said, looking behind him.

'Eyes to the left, Eddie,' Dad said. 'We've more important things to worry about than whether someone's following us or not.'

'Oh no,' Izzie said, as it grew darker.

'What is it?' said Eddie.

'If Cornflake camouflages himself we'll

have no chance of spotting him.'

'But at least that might mean no one else can spot him either,' Eddie said.

'And at least, for all its faults, Willow View is one of the tallest buildings around,' Dad said. 'A flying dragon might just be able to find our rooftop garden again.'

'Yes,' Izzie said, and Dad squeezed her hand. 'Oh, I so want him to come home.'

'Look!' Eddie said, as a dark shape came out of the shadows.

'Cornflake!' Izzie cried.

But it wasn't Cornflake. It was a cat and it ran across the road in front of them.

'What if a cat catches him?' Izzie said. She didn't want Cornflake to become cat prey.

'I think the cat would have a shock when

134

he breathed smoke – or fire,' said Eddie. 'And his skin is very tough.'

'Oh, yes,' said Izzie. At least Cornflake could protect himself a little bit and she was glad for that. 'But why did he go?'

'Maybe it was the call of the wild,' said Eddie. 'Drawing him away.'

But Izzie shook her head. 'I bet it was because he thought he was a problem. He thought it would be easier for us if he left.'

They searched for three hours, but they couldn't see the little dragon anywhere.

There was a rumble of thunder in the distance and finally Dad said, 'We have to go back. We'll come out to look for him as soon as it gets light, but now we all need some sleep.'

'I don't want to go home without him,' Izzie said.

'I don't either but it'll be light in a few hours and much easier to see him then,' Dad said, as he pressed the button for the lift.

'Everything all right?' Mrs Winters asked, coming out of her flat as they went past.

'No, it isn't,' said Izzie.

'Not all right at all,' said Eddie.

CHAPTER 17

As soon as they woke up, Eddie and Izzie headed out to look for Cornflake again. They were as quiet as they could be so they wouldn't wake Toby. But he woke up anyway and rubbed at his eyes.

'Dragons singing,' he said sleepily.

Eddie looked at Izzie and shrugged. 'What are you talking about?' he asked Toby.

'Everyone sleeping,' Toby said. 'But I heard it. Like Cornflake's song.'

Izzie shook her head. Toby must have dreamt it and thought it was real.

'You go back to sleep now,' she said, and Toby lay back down again and was almost instantly asleep again.

'It's only five o'clock,' Mum said, when they went into the lounge.

'We can't sleep,' said Eddie.

'We have to look for Cornflake,' said Izzie.

'I'll come and help too,' Dad said. 'Catch you up in a few minutes.'

'Where shall we look first?' Eddie said, when they stepped out of the lift on the ground floor.

Izzie bit her bottom lip. 'I've been

worrying that he might have fallen. He's only ever flown a little way above the roof before, and we're so high up.'

Eddie swallowed hard and nodded. 'Let's check all round the bottom of the flats first.'

Fortunately there was no one about because it was so early.

They made their way slowly and carefully round the blocks of flats. They looked in rubbish bins because they thought he might be hungry and looking for food, and at the bottom of outlet pipes in case he was thirsty. They searched everywhere, and all the time they could hardly breathe as they dreaded what they might find.

'There's no sign of him,' said Izzie.

'But we can't give up. Let's look this way now,' said Eddie.

Cornflake could be lying injured somewhere. Maybe he was just asleep. They had to look really carefully as he'd probably changed colour and blended in with his surroundings.

'Do you think he has red blood or a different colour, or maybe it changes when he changes colour . . .' Eddie said, and his voice trailed off at the thought of Cornflake hurt.

'Don't,' Izzie told him. 'Just don't think about it.'

'What's this?' Eddie said, and he picked up a pair of green glasses.

'They look like the ones the nosy parker wears,' Izzie said.

'But why would he have dropped them

and not picked them up?' Eddie asked her.

'Maybe he was running ... Running after something – trying to catch it!' Izzie said, as she had a horrible thought that made her blood run cold.

'Do you think he caught Cornflake?' Eddie said, and now they were both even more worried. Really, really worried.

'He could hurt him ...'

'Or sell him ...'

'They'd keep him in a cage for ever ... or worse.'

An hour later, they'd been all round the

flats and back again twice with no luck at all, and they headed home.

Mum made them toast but they couldn't eat it. Dad was still out looking.

'What if someone's taken him?' Izzie said. 'I'm sure the nosy parker's got something to do with it.'

'Where's Cornflake?' Toby asked, as he yawned his way into the kitchen. Then he remembered what had happened. 'Did you find him?'

Izzie shook her head.

'You have to find him,' Toby cried. 'You have to!'

Eddie and Izzie went out again to look, even though it seemed hopeless.

But they looked and looked and looked

and they couldn't find Cornflake anywhere.

'He's not coming back,' Izzie said. She'd have given anything to have Cornflake home again.

'I just hope he's all right wherever he is,' said Eddie.

CHAPTER 18

Eddie and Izzie didn't want to go back to school on Monday.

'Do we really have to go to school today, Mum?' asked Eddie. 'Couldn't we just stay home and look for Cornflake some more?'

Mum shook her head. 'You'll have to go sometime and it might as well be today,' she said. 'Take Cornflake's tank with you.

It'd be no use even if he does come back.'

'Do you think he might?' Izzie asked. 'I so want him to.'

'I know you do,' Mum said. 'I miss him too. It doesn't feel right without him here.'

'He was part of our family,' said Eddie.

'Dragon brother,' Toby said solemnly.

Mrs Winters was just getting into the lift as Eddie and Izzie headed towards it. She was holding two suitcases and had a bag slung over her shoulder.

'Hurry up, you two,' she shouted as she held the lift for them.

Eddie and Izzie hurried.

'Going on holiday, Mrs Winters?' Izzie asked her.

'Nope, I'm moving,' Mrs Winters said.

'Moving!' said Eddie.

'Where are you going?' Izzie asked.

'To my sister Ruby's,' Mrs Winters told her. 'She runs a home for stray cats.'

'I didn't know you liked cats,' said Eddie.

'We didn't think you liked any pets,' Izzie said.

'Whatever made you think that?' Mrs Winters said, looking surprised.

'Because you were going to report us when you thought we had one,' said Izzie.

'And we'd have been evicted,' added Eddie.

'Rules are rules,' Mrs Winters said, 'but that doesn't mean I don't like animals. I had to give my cat Flossy to my sister to look after when I came here, and when I saw you buying cat food it made me so sad and angry because I miss her so much. My sister could do with some help these days so I'm off to give her just that.'

'I'm glad.' Izzie smiled and Mrs Winters smiled back, although it looked like her face wasn't used to smiling. 'I'll miss you,' Izzie said.

Mrs Winters looked at her. 'You know, you can be quite thoughtful at times, especially for a child. If you did have a pet I'm sure you would take very good care of it. You too, Eddie.'

'Thanks,' Eddie said. It was the nicest thing Mrs Winters had ever said to them.

'Give Flossy a stroke from us,' Eddie said, as the lift stopped on the ground floor and Mrs Winters headed out to her waiting taxi.

'I will,' said Mrs Winters. 'And if you do ever decide to get a cat – well, there's not much I don't know about them.'

But they didn't want to get a cat – they wanted Cornflake.

CHAPTER 19

At school, Eddie and Izzie's class was buzzing with all the children chatting and laughing. Those who had been looking after pets had brought them back, and parents were there too, helping to bring in hutches and bedding and pet food.

'Straw in the corner, please,' Miss Harper told one of the parents.

Eddie put the empty tank on Miss Harper's desk.

'Excuse me, Miss,' Izzie said, but Miss Harper didn't hear her.

'No, no, no,' she said. 'Reptile tanks one side, mice cages the other.'

'We're sorry,' Eddie said.

Miss Harper looked at the empty tank. 'Oh, well, it was a very old lizard,' she said. 'These things happen. I did say it might not wake up one day.'

Eddie and Izzie kept hearing people talking about the pets they'd looked after.

Jemma had looked after one of the rabbits. 'Bugs Bunny liked eating asparagus and cucumber and curly kale and radishes and turnips and apples and peas . . .'

Izzie looked over at Eddie. Cornflake had liked cornflakes so much he'd crawled into the packet with them. She wished he'd come back and eat some more.

'The stick insects laid eggs . . .'

'The grass snake escaped from its tank and we found it in the bathroom . . .'

'The hamster played on its wheel all the time . . .'

Eddie and Izzie both thought about Cornflake riding on the back of Toby's truck. And how Cornflake had almost flooded the flat when he worked out how to turn on the taps in the bath. And how one day Mrs Winters had nearly spotted him. And how he loved dancing. And birthday candles. But they could never tell Miss Harper anything about him. They could never tell anyone. And no one would believe them even if they did.

The bell rang for the start of school.

'Bottoms on seats, everyone,' said Miss Harper. 'Now I'd like all of you to write about what you did during the holidays.'

'I'm writing about Toby's birthday but making Cornflake a toy dragon instead of a real one,' Izzie whispered to Eddie.

Eddie chewed on his pen and thought about what he wanted to write. Then he wrote about going out on the roof and how much he'd liked looking after the library lizard. He didn't say the library lizard had turned into a dragon, but he thought that even if Cornflake had just stayed being a lizard, he'd still have liked having him as a pet.

CHAPTER 20

When Izzie and Eddie got home that afternoon, they were horrified to find they had a visitor – it was the nosy parker! He was drinking a mug of tea in the armchair with the wobbly leg that Cornflake had broken.

'What's he doing here?' Eddie said.

'Meet Alfonzo Smith. He's from the

Secret Animal Society,' Dad said.

'Never heard of it,' said Eddie suspiciously. He gave the nosy parker a hard stare.

'Good,' said Alfonzo. 'That's just the way we like it. If everyone knew about our society then it wouldn't be very secret, would it?'

He showed them his Secret Animal Society card. At the top the letters were woven around an eye.

'What does the Secret Animal Society do, exactly?' Izzie asked him.

'We find very rare creatures and protect them – often creatures that no one believes exist, either because they're now extinct, or they think they're mythological. Dragons, for instance,' Alfonzo said. His face went all crinkly as he smiled. 'We were alerted to the possibility of a dragon being in the area by a series of unusual questions from a local library computer.'

Eddie and Izzie looked at each other. That must have been when they went to the library!

'I asked people if they'd seen anything unusual, and most of the strange sightings seemed to be near your block of flats,'

Alfonzo continued. 'Someone reported smoke and flames on the roof. Someone else said they'd seen a flying cat. I felt sure a dragon was living in your flat, but we have to be careful. And we have to make sure that information about secret animals doesn't accidentally get into the wrong hands.'

'We'd never tell anyone,' Izzie said.

'Not on purpose,' said Eddie.

Alfonzo nodded. 'My job is to investigate secret animal sightings and see if they're real – most of the time they're not. But very occasionally they are and then my job changes from finding them to making sure they're safe.'

Toby came in, riding his green and yellow tractor and pulling his red truck behind him.

Cornflake was sitting in the truck! Eddie and Izzie could hardly believe their eyes.

'Cornflake!' Izzie cried.

'He's back!' said Eddie.

'*Brmm brmm*,' said Toby.

'Alfonzo brought him back so we could  say goodbye,' said Dad. 'He thinks he might have flown away because he didn't want to be a burden to us.'

'He wasn't a burden,' Izzie said.

'It's just that our flat's so small and he needs space,' Mum said.

'How did you find him?' Eddie asked Alfonzo.

Alfonzo pulled out a small black box from his pocket.

'Cornflake is a very fine baby dragon,' he said. 'A lonely baby dragon.'

'We did the best we could,' said Eddie.

'I know and I'm sure he likes you all very much but the truth is you're not dragons. All I did was play him the night song of two of the other dragons we have at the sanctuary and he flew to me straight away.'

'You've got other dragons!' Izzie said.

'It's almost impossible to believe all the different creatures we have living there,' Alfonzo smiled. 'Sometimes I have to pinch myself to believe it and I've worked there for years.'

'So was Cornflake unhappy living with us?' Izzie said.

'Oh no. I could tell at once that you'd taken very good care of him. Dragons are born looking like lizards. They can stay like that for years. They only grow into dragons if the conditions are right – when they feel happy and know that they can thrive. Don't worry. He'll have all the space he needs in our secret animal sanctuary, and we have two other dragons there who will be company for him.'

Eddie swallowed hard. He didn't want Cornflake to leave with Alfonzo, but he knew the flat wasn't the best place for the little dragon to live, however much they all loved him and would miss him. They could visit him at weekends and in the holidays. It wouldn't be the same as having him live with them but it would be better than nothing.

Cornflake blinked and then stood up, flapped his wings and flew up and onto Dad's lap.

'Dragons are wonderful creatures, but many people see rare creatures as a way to make some money by exhibiting them or, worse, donating them to science to be poked and prodded about,' Alfonzo said.

Eddie and Izzie looked at each other. That was just what they'd thought Alfonzo might do.

'This family is really quite exceptional,' Alfonzo said, but then he looked sad. 'The caretaker of our home for secret animals is just like you. He loves them all very much, but Noah's very old now and so sadly he's retiring. I don't know how we're going to replace him. It's very, very hard to find just the right sort of people for this work. They need to have only the best interests of the creatures we look after at heart and also be able to keep them secret.'

'Our dad could do it,' said Eddie.

'Yes, he could,' Izzie agreed.

'I've never worked with unusual sorts of animals before,' Dad said.

'But you've helped lots of different sorts of *real* animals, Dad,' said Eddie. 'You always help them when you can.' He told Alfonzo about the time his dad had helped to rescue a cat that had got stuck on a roof. And the time he'd shown him how to carefully put the baby birds' nest back after it had fallen during a storm. They'd kept watch until the bird parents came back. Any time his

dad saw an animal – or a person – in need, he helped if he could. It was just the way he was.

'There's not much difference between secret animals and real ones,' Alfonzo said. 'All they need is love and kindness mixed in with a good dollop of common sense.'

'Will any of them be dangerous?' Mum asked. 'Toby's still very young.'

'No, I'm not – I'm three,' Toby said.

'That's where the common sense will come in,' Alfonzo said. 'We wouldn't want any of you to be in danger. Some of the animals will be very frightened and may not be as friendly as Cornflake.'

He looked at Cornflake, who'd hopped off Dad's lap to be with the children. The little dragon was looking up at him with his head tilted to one side.

'So he'd be looking after secret animals, rather than farm ones or pets?' Mum said.

'Yes,' Alfonzo said. 'Perhaps you can all help out. You might also want to accompany me on missions to find the animals. That would be very useful.'

'Sounds just amazing,' Dad said. 'The perfect job.'

Izzie couldn't remember seeing him this happy in a long, long time. She saw Eddie looking at him too and smiled.

'Would you really be interested?' Alfonzo asked. 'It would be wonderful if you were, although it would mean moving away from your flat. You'd have to live next to the sea because there are lots of secret creatures there. But we'd provide a house, and it wouldn't ever be boring!'

'Sounds wonderful,' said Mum, squeezing Dad's hand. Dad looked like he still couldn't quite believe it.

Toby went into the bedroom and came out again dragging his suitcase.

'When can we go?' he said, opening the lid.

'Soon as you like,' said Alfonzo. 'The sooner the better.'

'It's like a dream come true,' said Eddie. He couldn't wait to meet all the different secret animals.

Cornflake flew around the room and landed on the suitcase.

Izzie smiled. 'And all thanks to the grumpy school lizard!'

The Secret Animal Society

Don't miss the next exciting adventure of the
Secret Animal Society. . .

Spike the Sea Serpent

Twins Eddie and Izzie now live with their family
at the Secret Animal Society sanctuary, helping
to protect all sorts of very rare animals. A strange
creature has been sighted far out at sea. At first
everyone thinks it must be a shark or a whale,
but they soon realise it's Spike – a sea serpent
related to the Loch Ness Monster, who no one has
seen for years. Spike is obviously in distress –
but what's wrong?

Available from all good bookshops and online in March 2015

ISBN: 978-1-84812-446-2

www.secretanimalsociety.com

www.piccadillypress.co.uk